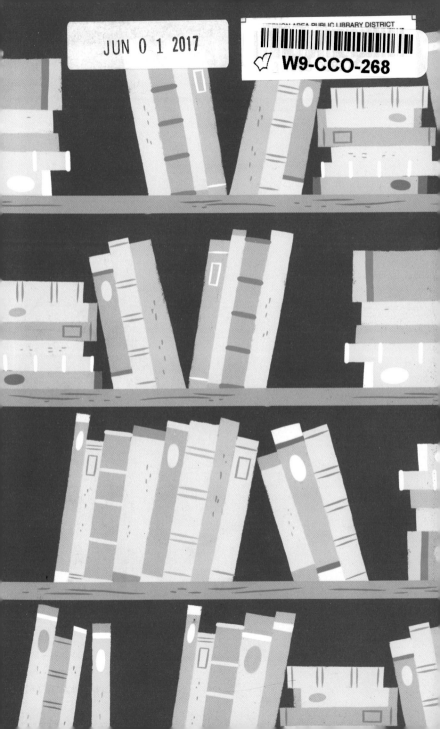

The HAUNTED LIBRARY

FOR THE REAL
UNCLE DAVE
—DHB

* * * * * * * * * * * * * * * *

GROSSET & DUNLAP
Penguin Young Readers Group
An Imprint of Penguin Random House LLC

Penguin supports copyright. Copyright fuels creativity, encourages diverse voices, promotes free speech, and creates a vibrant culture. Thank you for buying an authorized edition of this book and for complying with copyright laws by not reproducing, scanning, or distributing any part of it in any form without permission. You are supporting writers and allowing Penguin to continue to publish books for every reader.

Text copyright © 2017 by Dori Hillestad Butler. Illustrations copyright © 2017 by Aurore Damant. All rights reserved. Published by Grosset & Dunlap, an imprint of Penguin Random House LLC, 345 Hudson Street, New York, New York 10014. GROSSET & DUNLAP is a trademark of Penguin Random House LLC. Printed in the USA.

Library of Congress Cataloging-in-Publication Data is available.

ISBN 9780451534354 (pbk)   10 9 8 7 6 5 4 3 2 1
ISBN 9780451534361 (hc)   10 9 8 7 6 5 4 3 2 1

The HAUNTED LIBRARY

THE GHOSTS AT THE MOVIE THEATER

BY DORI HILLESTAD BUTLER
ILLUSTRATED BY AURORE DAMANT

GROSSET & DUNLAP * AN IMPRINT OF PENGUIN RANDOM HOUSE

GHOSTLY GLOSSARY

EXPAND
When ghosts make themselves larger

GLOW
What ghosts do so humans can see them

HAUNT
Where ghosts live

PASS THROUGH
When ghosts travel through walls, doors, and other solid objects

SHRINK
When ghosts make themselves smaller

SKIZZY
When ghosts feel sick to their stomachs

SOLIDS
What ghosts call humans

SPEW
Ghostly vomit

SWIM
When ghosts move freely through the air

TRANSFORMATION
When a ghost takes a solid object and turns it into a ghostly object

WAIL
What ghosts do so humans can hear them

CHAPTER 1

A BIG FAVOR

"Y ou guys! Come quick!" Little John shouted as he swam into Claire's living room. "You won't believe what Finn is doing!"

It was the middle of the night. Kaz, Cosmo, Mom, Pops, Grandmom, and Grandpop had the TV on, but they weren't paying much attention to it. They just had it on while they waited for Claire to wake up. The ghosts had a big favor to ask of Claire.

Kaz groaned. "What's Finn doing?" he asked his younger brother, Little John.

Finn was Kaz and Little John's big brother. Back when the ghosts lived in the old schoolhouse, Finn liked to scare his brothers by putting an arm, leg, or his head through the outside wall. One day he pushed his head too far through the wall and he got stuck in the Outside. Grandmom and Grandpop tried to rescue him, but the wind blew them all away.

A few months later, some solids came and tore down the old schoolhouse. Kaz and the rest of his family were forced into the Outside. The wind blew them away, too. It blew Kaz to the library, where he met Claire, the solid girl who lives above the library with her parents and her grandma.

Kaz didn't think he'd ever see the rest

of his family again. But he and Claire found Cosmo when they were searching for a ghost in an attic. Little John had gotten himself "returned" to the library inside a book. The three of them found Grandmom and Grandpop at a nursing home. They found Mom and Pops at a girl named Margaret's house. And just yesterday, they found Finn at a boy named Eli's house.

"You have to *see* what Finn's doing," Little John said. "He's in Claire's room."

Kaz sighed. Whatever Finn was doing in Claire's room in the middle of the night, it couldn't be good.

The ghosts swam down the hall and through Claire's bedroom door. Claire was sound asleep on her bed, and Finn was braiding her hair to the bedpost!

Kaz gasped. "Finn!"

"Woof! Woof!" Cosmo barked at
Finn while Mom, Pops, Grandmom, and
Grandpop shook their heads in disapproval.

"You're such a tattletale, Little John,"
Finn said.

"Come on, Finn," Kaz said. "That's not
very nice."

All of a sudden, Claire jerked awake.
She tried to sit up, but couldn't. "What
the—?" she said. Her fingers followed her
hair all the way to the bedpost.

"Who did this?" she asked the ghosts. Her gaze settled on Finn. She made a face at him.

"Aw, can't you take a joke?" Finn asked. He tried to help Claire unbraid her hair, but she didn't want his help. She shoved her hand through his chest.

"Way to go, Finn," Little John said. "Claire may not want to do us that favor now."

"What favor?" Claire asked as her hair came free from the bedpost.

"She can't do it in the middle of the night," Kaz said. "Go back to sleep, Claire. We'll ask you in the morning." Maybe by then she will have forgotten what Finn did to her hair.

Claire turned on her bedside lamp. "I'm awake now," she said, combing her hair with her fingers. "Go ahead and ask."

The ghosts looked at one another. Mom motioned for Kaz to do the asking.

"Well . . ." Kaz wafted closer to Claire. "You know how there's this little problem between our family and Beckett?"

Beckett was the other ghost who lived at the library. For some reason, Mom, Grandmom, and Grandpop never wanted to be in the same room with Beckett. So they made a deal: Beckett would stay in the library and the other ghosts would stay in Claire's apartment. Tonight Mom, Grandmom, and Grandpop finally told

Kaz, Finn, and Little John *why* there was a problem between Beckett and their family.

And now Kaz was explaining it to Claire. "When our mom and Beckett were young ghosts, Beckett lived with her family for a while," he began.

"He did?" Claire said, hugging her knees to her chest.

"Yes," Kaz said. "You know how we've never seen Beckett glow?"

Little John couldn't wait for Kaz to finish telling the story. "Beckett doesn't glow blue like we do," he blurted. "He glows red!"

"Really?" Claire gaped at the ghosts. "I've never heard of a ghost who glows red."

"Wait, there's more," Kaz said. "Our mom had a little brother named Dave.

One day Beckett glowed, and his red glow scared Dave so bad that he jumped right through the wall of their haunt, and the wind blew him away. They haven't seen him since."

Finn picked up the story from there. "Remember when I said I was at the movie theater before I was at Eli's house? Well, there's a ghost named Dave there. We want you to take us to the movie theater so we can find out if he's Mom's long-lost brother!"

"Maybe if we find Dave, then you guys will forgive Beckett for what happened and we can all be friends," Kaz said to his mom and grandparents.

"Maybe," Grandmom and Grandpop said. But they made no promises.

Claire thought about the situation. "Okay," she said, stifling a yawn.

"Tomorrow's Saturday. I think the movie theater opens at one. How about we go right after lunch?" Then she lay down, pulled the covers over her head, and went back to sleep.

* * * * * * * * * * * * *

Everyone in Kaz's family wanted to go to the movie theater. That was eight ghosts, including Cosmo. Unfortunately, Claire's water bottle only held four ghosts comfortably. Five if they shrank extra small and squished together.

"I don't have to go if there isn't room," Pops said.

"Me either," Kaz said. He thought Finn should go because Finn was the one who knew the ghost at the movie theater. And Mom, Grandmom, and Grandpop should go because Uncle Dave was Mom's brother, and Grandmom and Grandpop's son.

"Little John, Pops, and I could stay here with Cosmo," Kaz said as he put his arm around Little John.

"Woof! Woof!" Cosmo barked.

"No, Kaz," Claire said. "You have to come. We're C & K Detectives. We're a team."

Little John ducked out from under Kaz's arm. "I'm C & K Detectives, too!" he said, even though his name didn't start with C *or* K. "I've helped you solve cases.

I want to see if Finn's friend is our Uncle Dave, too."

"You should all come," Claire said. "I'll find something big enough to hold you all."

The ghosts followed Claire into the kitchen. She scanned the counters, then opened the fridge. "How about this?" she said, reaching for an almost empty bottle of orange juice. She finished what was left, then rinsed the bottle in the sink.

"Perfect," Kaz said as he grabbed his dog. The ghosts shrank down . . . down . . . down . . . and passed through the bottle.

"I'm going to the movies," Claire called to her family.

Claire's mom poked her head out of her office. "What are you going to see?" she asked. Claire's parents were detectives, too—just like Claire and Kaz. But Claire's parents solved regular mysteries, and Claire and Kaz solved ghostly mysteries.

"I don't know. Whatever's showing," Claire said with a shrug. "I'm only going because there's a ghost at the movie theater and we want to find out if it's Kaz's long-lost uncle. I've got his whole family in here." She tapped the orange juice bottle.

Even though Claire's mom couldn't see Kaz and his family, she knew all about them. So did Claire's dad and Grandma Karen. In fact, Claire's mom and grandma could see ghosts when they were Claire's

age, too. But Claire's dad has never been able to see ghosts.

"Okay, but be back in time for dinner," her mom said.

"I will," Claire promised.

* * * * * * * * * * * * * * * * *

The movie theater was downtown, right in the middle of a block. There was a toy store on one side of the theater and a Mexican restaurant on the other. Claire went inside the theater and got in line to buy a ticket for the movie.

THEATER

THE MONSTER OF THE LAKE
LOVE IS ALL

MEXICAN

"Hey, look! It's Conrad, Jessie, and George!" Finn said as he passed through the bottle. The rest of the family had no idea who Conrad, Jessie, and George were, but they followed Finn through the bottle and across the large open room.

They saw three new ghosts hovering above a brightly lit snack counter where some solid people were buying popcorn. Two of the ghosts were teenagers—a boy and a girl. They were holding hands and looking at each other all googly-eyed. The other ghost was younger. Not as young as Little John, but younger than Kaz.

The three ghosts turned. "Finn!" they shrieked. They swam over and threw their arms around Finn.

Grandpop cleared his throat. "Finn? Are you going to introduce us to your friends?"

18

"Oh, sorry," Finn said. He gestured toward the teenagers. "This is Jessie and Conrad. The little one's George. Guys, this is my mom and dad, my grandparents, my brothers, Kaz and Little John, and my dog, Cosmo."

"Woof! Woof!" Cosmo barked.

"Aw," Jessie said. "You found your family!"

"Cool," Conrad said, shaking hands with everyone.

"Where's Dave?" Mom asked, looking all around.

"You know Dave?" George asked as Conrad and Jessie exchanged a look.

"What?" Finn said. "What's that look?"

"Dude," Conrad said in a low voice as Claire joined the crowd of ghosts. "I hate to break this to you, but Dave's gone."

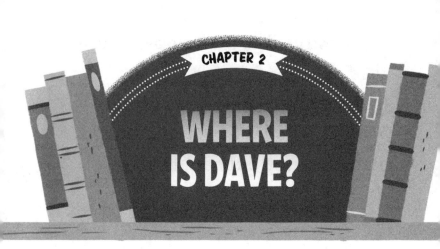

CHAPTER 2

WHERE IS DAVE?

one?!" Mom exclaimed.

Grandpop wafted forward.

"What do you mean gone?"

"I mean *gone*. Disappeared. Not here anymore," Conrad said.

"Where'd he go?" Grandmom asked.

"We have no idea," Jessie said.

Claire set her orange juice bottle on the floor and pulled a purple notebook and green pen from her bag. She glanced warily at the other solid people who were

buying popcorn at the counter, then turned her back to them. "How long has Dave been gone?" she asked Finn's friends.

George's mouth fell open. Jessie and Conrad waved their hands in Claire's face. "Can you see us?"

"Yes. I can hear you, too," Claire said, barely moving her lips. She was used to ghosts asking her these questions.

"How?" Conrad and Jessie asked.

"We're not glowing," George said.

Claire shrugged as two solid girls walked past her with their popcorn.

"No one knows," Little John said.

"Someone must know," Jessie said. "There must be some explanation."

Claire shrugged again.

"What's the matter? Cat got your tongue?" Conrad asked.

"She doesn't like to talk a lot when

all these other people are around," Kaz explained. "They can't see us, so they'll think she's talking to herself."

"Ohhh," Conrad and Jessie said at the same time.

"Let's talk about Dave instead of Claire," Kaz said. "How long has he been gone?"

"Since yesterday," Conrad said.

Kaz glanced out the big front window at the stores across the street. A ghost could pass through walls and visit a bunch of stores on that side of the street without ever going outside. You could probably do that on this side of the street, too.

"Maybe he's not really gone," Kaz said. "Isn't there a toy store on the other side of that wall?" He pointed to the wall behind the snack counter. "And a restaurant on the other side of that wall?" He pointed to the

other wall. "Maybe Dave's in one of the other stores or restaurants on this block."

"We already looked in all the other stores on this block," George said.

"Several times," Conrad said. "He's gone."

"We know he's gone because he didn't show up for the sing-along last night," Jessie said.

"Sing-along?" Little John asked.

"You guys still do that?" Finn asked.

"Of course," Jessie replied. She turned to the other ghosts. "After the theater closes, we meet by the piano in the balcony and have a sing-along."

"It's how we celebrate that all the solids have gone home for the night," Conrad added.

"My brother always loved music," Mom said with a wistful smile.

"He did indeed," Grandmom agreed as Claire wrote everything in her notebook.

"Dave wouldn't leave without saying good-bye," George said. "Something bad must've happened to him." Jessie and Conrad nodded in agreement.

"Maybe he accidentally passed through the back wall," Finn said. "If you pass through the back wall, you don't end up in another store. You end up in the Outside. In an alley. That's what happened to me."

"Tell us about it," Pops said to Finn.

"Well," Finn said, looking a little embarrassed. "I was making faces at the solids before the movie started. Just for fun. And I sort of backed through the wall into the Outside. The wind blew me into a packing and shipping store across the alley. I tried to swim back over here, but the wind was too strong. It blew me up and over all these stores. I ended up at the library for a while. Then Eli's house. That's where Kaz and Little John found me."

"Maybe the wind blew Dave to Eli's house, too," Little John suggested.

"I think it's more likely that it blew him into one of the stores across the alley," Finn said.

"We can go around the block and see if he's in any of the stores over there," Claire said. By now most of the other solid people in the lobby had gone into the theater.

"Yes, let's do that," Mom said as a solid man in a wheelchair rolled right through her.

The solid man wore black pants, a black jacket over a white shirt, and a name tag that said Irwin. "The movie is about to start," he told Claire. "You

might want to go find a seat." He couldn't see the eleven ghosts hovering around him.

"I changed my mind," Claire said, closing her notebook. "I don't think I can stay for the movie after all."

"But you just bought a ticket," Irwin said. "What's the matter? Are you sick?"

"Uh . . . yes!" Claire said. She clutched her stomach. "I mean, I think I might be getting sick."

Irwin rolled backward. "Well, save your ticket. Then you can come back and see the movie another day."

"I will. Thanks." Claire stuffed her notebook back in her bag and zipped it up.

Kaz and his family shrank down . . . down . . . down . . . and swam into the empty orange juice bottle at Claire's feet. Luckily, no one had noticed it.

"That's an interesting way to travel," Conrad said, peering in at all the ghosts.

"You want to come with us?" Finn asked.

"It looks a little crowded," Jessie said, holding tight to Conrad's hand.

"We'll stay here in case Dave comes back," George said.

"Don't worry. We'll find him," Little John said as Claire picked up the bottle.

"And when we do, we'll bring him back here," Finn added.

Would they? Kaz wondered. He thought they'd bring Dave to the library.

* * * * * * * * * * * *

"There are so many buildings," Mom said as Claire walked the ghosts around the block. "Dave could be anywhere. I don't know how we'll ever find him."

"We don't even know if the Dave from the movie theater is *our* Dave," Grandmom said.

"I think he is," Finn said.

Claire stopped in front of a dark store. "This must be the packing and shipping store you blew into, Finn."

"Yup," Finn said. He read the writing on the front window out loud. "'Pack Mack. You pack. We ship.' This is the place. Let's go in."

"There aren't any lights on in there,"

Kaz said. "Are they open?"

"They should be. The sign says they're open from nine until five on Saturdays," Pops said.

Claire tried the door. It was locked. "Oh, there's a note on the door," she said. "Closed today for family emergency. Sorry for the inconvenience."

"That is *really* inconvenient," Finn said with a huff.

"Well, Claire can't go inside. But if she puts the bottle a little closer to the window, the rest of us can go in," Little John said.

"That's true," Finn said, looking more hopeful. "In fact, we can pass through the walls and search all the stores on this block."

"There's a bakery at the other end of the block," Claire said. "I'll meet you down there."

"Are you sure the bakery is open?" Kaz asked.

Claire craned her neck. "Yes, I can see lights on from here."

"Then let's go!" Little John said.

Claire held the bottle up against the window and one by one, the ghosts passed through the bottle and the glass window and went inside the packing and shipping store. Kaz and Cosmo were the last ones through.

"See you in a little bit!" Claire waved good-bye, then skipped down the street.

"Hello? Dave, are you in here?" Finn called as the ghosts spread out around the store. There was a large counter in the middle of the room. Brown wrapping paper, packing material, and boxes of all different sizes and shapes lined the shelves.

Finn and Mom swam into a back room. Kaz, Cosmo, and Pops floated along the dimly lit shelves. Little John poked his head into several of the boxes. Grandmom and Grandpop passed through the cabinets that lined the back wall.

None of them found any other ghosts.

"Let's try the next store," Finn said when he and Mom returned from the

back room. He led the others through the side wall and into a fancy restaurant with white tablecloths and gold candles on all the tables.

There were no other ghosts in there, either, so Kaz and his family continued on to the hardware store. Then a bank. The last store on the block was the bakery. Claire was already there when Kaz entered through a side wall.

Claire was talking to a man who wore a white apron around his thick middle and a tall hat on his head. He stood behind a glass case that was full of cookies, cakes, and donuts. A rack of cookies cooled on the counter behind him.

"Oh, yes," the man said in a serious voice. "We have a ghost in here. You bet we do."

CHAPTER 3
ANOTHER NEW GHOST?

eally?" Claire set her orange juice bottle on the floor while Kaz and his family looked around. They didn't see any ghosts.

"Have you actually seen this ghost with your very own eyes?" Claire asked the baker.

"I sure have," he replied. "Many times."

"Can you see *us*?" Finn asked.

Little John wiggled his fingers and stuck out his tongue. Grandmom and Grandpop waved their hands in the baker's face.

The baker didn't even blink. He picked up a towel and started wiping the counter.

"He can't see us," Grandpop said.

"That means Dave was glowing!" Little John said.

"If Dave was actually here," Kaz put in.

"Why would Dave glow?" Mom asked. "Why would he want this solid man to see him?"

"There are lots of reasons ghosts glow, Mom," Finn said.

Claire took out her notebook. "When did you see this ghost?" she asked.

"This morning. Yesterday morning. I see him almost every morning," the baker replied.

"Then it's not Dave," Finn said. "Dave's only been missing since yesterday."

"The Dave from the movie theater has only been missing since yesterday," Little John pointed out. "This ghost could still be *our* Dave."

Kaz scratched his head. They were looking for a ghost named Dave. But was there one ghost named Dave or were there two? Was the Dave from the movie theater and Mom's long-lost brother, Dave, the same ghost? This was confusing.

Little John cupped his hand around his mouth and called, "Hello, Ghost?

Where are you? Come out, come out wherever you are!"

"There's another room back there," Finn said, straining to see through a small window in a door behind the baker. "It looks like a kitchen."

"Let's go see if Dave is in there," Mom said as she and Finn sailed up and over the baker's head.

"Wait for me!" Little John cried. He followed Mom and Finn through the door.

Kaz and the others stayed where they were.

Claire opened to a new page in her notebook. "So, it's a boy ghost," she said as she started to draw a ghost.

"Yes," the baker said.

"Can you describe him?"

"Sure," the baker said. "He looks like a ghost!"

Grandpop snorted. "That's helpful."

Claire looked up from her drawing. "Is he young or old?"

"Youngish," the baker replied.

"What was he wearing?" Claire asked.

The baker laughed. "Silly. Ghosts don't wear clothes!"

"We don't?" Grandpop said, snapping the straps on his suspenders. "Since when?"

Mom, Finn, and Little John returned from the kitchen. "We didn't find any ghosts in there, either," Little John said.

"Can you describe the ghost's hair?" Claire asked the baker. "Is it long? Short? Curly? Straight?"

The baker laughed again. "You have some funny ideas about ghosts," he said as he folded his towel and set it on the counter. "They don't have hair!"

Finn clucked his tongue. "This guy doesn't think we have hair?"

"He doesn't think we wear clothes, either," Kaz said.

Claire tipped her head to the side. "Are you sure you've seen a ghost in here?" she asked.

"Yes!" The baker picked up a pan of cookies and a spatula and started putting the cookies in the display case. "But I don't think *you've* ever seen one, young lady." He waved the spatula at Claire. "So let me tell you about them. First, ghosts don't look anything like us. They look like floating white sheets with black holes for their eyes, noses, and mouths."

Pops crossed his arms. "There's no way this man has seen a ghost."

"We could change that," Little John said, rubbing his hands together.

"I think we *should* change that," Finn said.

"Oh, no," Kaz said.

"On three," Finn said with a grin. "Ready? One . . . two . . . three!"

The whole family (even Cosmo!) started to glow. Everyone but Kaz.

The pan of cookies slipped from the baker's hand and clattered to the floor. His face was as white as his apron and his hat. "Wh-wh-what's happening?" he stammered, his eyes flicking from ghost to ghost to ghost.

"What do you mean?" Claire asked innocently. She acted as though she couldn't see the glowing ghosts in front of her.

Kaz had never wanted to glow so badly as he did that second. He tightened his hands into fists and gritted his teeth—even though he knew that was wrong—and he tried, tried, *tried* to glow with the rest of his family. But as usual, nothing happened.

"I-I'm not feeling so good," the baker moaned. Leaving the pan and broken cookies scattered on the floor, he backed through the swinging door behind him and disappeared into the kitchen.

"Should we follow him?" Little John asked.

"No," Pops said as the glow faded from his body. "I think we've made our point."

The other ghosts stopped glowing, too.

"Let's go back to the library and figure out what our next step should be," Kaz said.

"If you don't mind," Grandpop said to Claire, "perhaps you could drop Eva

and me at the nursing home on your way."

"You don't want to come back to the library with us?" Mom asked.

"What about Dave?" Finn said. "Don't you want to help us find Dave?"

"You have to understand," Grandmom said, squeezing Finn's arm, "Dave has been gone a long time."

"That's right," Grandpop said. "It's nice to think that your friend Dave might be our long-lost son, but we don't know that. All we know is now *he's* gone, too."

Grandmom nodded. "We're too old for all this running around," she said. "If you find your friend, or any other ghost named Dave, you'll come to the nursing home and let us know, won't you?"

"Of course," Claire replied.

"Then we'd like to go back to Valley View," Grandmom said.

43

"I don't blame you," Mom said, patting Grandmom's arm. "You've been away from your friends there for a long time."

Grandmom and Grandpop had only come to the library for a visit after Claire and Kaz had found Mom and Pops. They never planned to stay permanently.

"I'll take you back to Valley View right now," Claire said.

The ghosts shrank down . . . down . . . down . . . and swam inside her empty orange juice bottle.

"Um, good-bye!" Claire called to the baker in the kitchen. "I hope you feel better soon." She grabbed her bottle of ghosts and left the bakery. She walked Grandmom and Grandpop back to Valley View. Then she took everyone else back to the library.

CHAPTER 4

HOW DO YOU FIND A MISSING GHOST?

laire hugged her orange juice bottle of ghosts with one arm while she opened the door to the library with her other hand.

Beckett hovered in the library entryway, close to the front door, but not so close that he might blow into the Outside. "Well? Did you find Dave?" he asked hopefully.

"No," Claire said, kicking the door closed behind her.

"What happened?" Beckett asked as Kaz, Cosmo, Finn, and Little John passed through the bottle and expanded to their normal sizes. He backed away when Mom and Pops passed through.

"We met some of Finn's friends," Little John said. "But not Dave. Dave's gone."

"Gone!" Beckett said.

"Yeah. No one knows what happened to him," Kaz said. "We looked for him in a bunch of stores and restaurants downtown. So did the other ghosts at the movie theater—"

"Wait, there are other ghosts at the movie theater?" Beckett said, scratching his head.

"Yes," Finn said. "Jessie, Conrad, George, and Dave. Dave used to be there. I just don't know what could have happened to him."

"It's a mystery all right," Little John said.

Beckett peered into the empty

orange juice bottle. "Where are your grandparents?" he asked. "Did something happen to them, too?"

"No. I took them back to Valley View," Claire said as she wiggled out of her jacket.

"They're old. And tired," Mom said. She sounded pretty tired herself. "They don't think we'll ever find my brother. Frankly, I don't think we will, either." With that, she and Pops drifted up through the ceiling.

"I'm so sorry," Beckett said, hanging his head.

"Come on," Claire said to Kaz, Finn, and Little John as she headed for the craft room. Kaz picked up Cosmo, and the ghosts followed Claire.

"We *will* find your Uncle Dave!" Claire declared. She pulled out a chair and sat down.

"How?" Kaz asked. "He's been gone forever!"

"We can start by finding my friend, Dave," Finn said. "He's only been gone a day. If we can find him, we can at least find out whether he's our Uncle Dave."

"How are we going to find him?" Kaz asked. "Have Claire knock on every door in this whole town until we find him? There are too many."

"He may not even be in this town anymore," Little John said. "The wind may have blown him to a whole different town."

"You sound like you're giving up," Claire said to Little John. "I've never known *you* to give up before."

Little John bit his lip. "Well, it does seem kind of impossible," he said in a small voice.

Claire leaned back in her chair. "You guys! We found your whole family! You thought that was impossible, too. But we did it."

"I'm not giving up," Finn said, folding his arms. "If they want to give up, maybe you need to change the name of your little detective agency to C & F Ghost Detectives."

C & F Ghost Detectives? No way, Kaz thought. "I'm not giving up, either," he said. "I just don't know what to do."

"Same," Little John said.

"Well," Claire said as she unzipped her bag and pulled out her notebook and pen. "I like Finn's idea of looking for his friend, Dave. It's a lot easier to find someone who's

49

only been missing for a day rather than someone who's been missing for years and years. If he's your long-lost uncle, the case is solved. If he's not, well . . . then we'll have to figure out what to do next."

Kaz wasn't sure he agreed that it was any easier to find someone who's only been missing for a day. "So how do we find him?" he asked again.

"We could put up flyers like people do when they're trying to find a lost dog," Claire suggested.

"Woof! Woof!" Cosmo barked when he heard the word *dog*.

"It could say, 'Have you seen this ghost? If so, call C & K Detectives,'" Claire went on.

"Who's going to call and say 'yeah, I saw that ghost'?" Finn asked. "Most solids aren't

like you. They can't see ghosts."

"They can if the ghost is glowing," Claire reminded him.

"That boy Eli called Claire because you kept glowing around him," Little John pointed out.

"True," Finn said.

Claire turned to a clean sheet of paper in her notebook and said, "What does your friend Dave look like, Finn?"

"I bet he has hair and wears clothes," Kaz said.

Finn snorted. "He definitely wears clothes. I can't say much about his hair. It's covered up by a baseball cap."

"What else?" Claire asked as she drew a man with a baseball cap.

Finn peered over Claire's shoulder. "Oh, he's bigger than that. His stomach is like this." Finn cupped his hands around

his own stomach to show Claire how big Dave's stomach was. "And he wears a T-shirt and jeans."

Claire kept drawing.

"That's good!" Finn said. "It really looks like Dave."

Claire ripped the page from her notebook, then pushed back her chair. "Let's go make copies of this. Tomorrow we can put them up around town."

* * * * * * * * * * * * * * * * * *

The next day, Kaz, Finn, and Little John
traveled with Claire inside her water bottle.
Their parents stayed at the library with
Cosmo.

Claire pinned flyers to bulletin boards
inside grocery stores and coffee shops. She
stapled them to trees and utility poles. She
taped them to windows and mailboxes.

"Who knew this town was so big?" Finn said, drifting to the bottom of Claire's water bottle. "I'm exhausted!"

"*You're* exhausted?" Claire said to Finn. "You're not the one who's been walking all over." She set her water bottle down on the sidewalk outside the movie theater while she taped another poster to a large mailbox by the window.

"If you're so tired, maybe we should go inside and watch a movie," Little John said.

"That's actually a good idea," Finn said. "We could find out if Dave came back!"

"Why not?" Claire said. She picked up her water bottle and went inside the movie theater.

CHAPTER 5

MORE MISSING GHOSTS

The doors to the movie theater stood wide open, so the ghosts didn't dare pass through Claire's water bottle until they were farther into the lobby area.

"Excuse me, Miss?" A solid lady at the ticket counter called to Claire. "Do you have a ticket?"

Claire stopped. "Oh. Yes, I do," she said. She opened the front pocket of her bag and pulled out a paper ticket.

The lady looked at it over the tops of her glasses. "Thank you," she said.

There were no ghosts in the lobby today. And the only solid people were the guy behind the snack counter and Irwin, the man who had told Claire to save her ticket when she left yesterday.

"Looks like you're feeling better today." He smiled when Claire approached.

"Yes, much better," Claire said as she handed him her ticket.

Irwin tore it in half. "Enjoy the show!" he said.

The ghosts passed through the bottle and followed Claire down a dim hallway. Little John hovered beside a poster of a five-eyed monster on the wall. He gulped. "Is that the movie that's showing?"

"You're not scared to see that movie, are you, Little John?" Finn asked.

"No!" Little John said right away. "Are *you* scared to see it, Kaz?"

"No," Kaz said. And he wasn't. Well, not *too* scared, anyway. "It's just a movie. Plus we're here to see if Dave came back. Where are your friends, Finn? I don't see them anywhere."

"They're probably in the theater," Finn said.

Claire yanked open the door and went into the dark theater. Kaz and his brothers wafted in behind her.

The movie had already started. Loud, scary music pulsed from speakers on the wall as Claire sat down. Kaz tried not to look at the monster on the screen, but he couldn't not look. The monster really did have five eyes, just like on the poster.

"The ghosts aren't in here, either!" Little John said, turning his back to the movie.

"Maybe we should go look for them," Kaz said.

"We should definitely go look for them," Little John said, swimming toward the door.

Claire leaned back in her chair. "Okay. Come back when you find them," she whispered to Kaz.

He nodded, then followed his brothers.

"I don't know where else they could be," Finn said. He looked up and down the dim hallway. The only person—solid or ghost—out here was Irwin.

"They could be in one of the other stores on this block," Kaz suggested. Maybe they didn't like scary movies any more than Little John did.

"Maybe," Finn said. "Or maybe they're in one of the bathrooms. Or upstairs in the projection room."

"Let's check the bathrooms," Little John said. He darted across the hall and into the men's room.

"Jessie? Conrad? George?" Finn called as the ghosts passed through the men's room door. "Are any of you in here?"

"I-I'm here," George said in a wobbly

voice. He wafted up above the stall door just high enough to peek over the top.

Finn laughed. "Did that movie scare you, George?"

"No," George said, shaking his head. "It w-wasn't the movie."

"Then what?" Kaz asked. "Where are Jessie and Conrad?"

George gulped. "A bad boy came and blew them away!" he said.

"WHAT?" Kaz, Finn, and Little John all said at once.

"It's true," George said. "He didn't see me. But he saw Jessie and Conrad. He's like your friend, the solid girl. No one was glowing, but that boy saw Jessie and Conrad anyway."

The ghosts looked at one another. There was *someone else* like Claire?

"We were playing that game we like to play," George said to Finn.

"You mean Solid Pass Through?" Finn said.

George nodded. "It's a game where you pick a spot anywhere in the lobby and you try not to move, and you see how many solid people will walk through you," he told Kaz and Little John.

"You don't get points if you accidentally pass through them," Finn added. "*They* have to walk through *you*."

"This boy walked right over to Jessie and Conrad," George said. "He had this *thing* in his hand. It was like a wind machine.

He turned it on and blew Jessie and Conrad right through the front window!"

"When did all this happen?" Kaz asked.

"Last night. After you guys left," George replied. "And then that guy who takes the tickets gave the boy some money. The way they were talking, it sounded like the ticket guy hired the boy to get rid of us!"

* * * * * * * * * * * * * * * *

Kaz, Finn, and Little John went to tell Claire what they'd just learned. George was too scared to leave the bathroom.

"There's someone else like me?" Claire gaped at the ghosts. "Someone who's not in my own family?"

The two solid people in the row ahead of Claire turned and glared. "Shh!" the woman hissed at her.

"Sorry," Claire whispered.

"Who's she talking to, anyway?" the man asked.

The woman shrugged. They couldn't see the three ghosts hovered around Claire.

Claire got up and followed Kaz, Little John, and Finn out of the theater. "I want to talk to George," she said.

"You can't," Little John said. "He's in the men's room and he won't come out."

"He's scared," Kaz said.

"Scared of solid people like you who can see ghosts when we're not glowing," Finn added.

Claire leaned against the wall and sighed.

Irwin turned his wheelchair and rolled it toward her. "Are you not feeling well again?" he asked.

"George said that guy hired the other

guy to get rid of the ghosts." Kaz pointed at Irwin. "Why don't you ask him about it, Claire."

Claire nodded slightly to show Kaz she'd heard him. "No, I'm fine," she told Irwin. "But I was wondering, have you ever seen any ghosts in here?"

"Ghosts!" Irwin exclaimed. "Are there more in here? Did you see them in the theater?" He frowned. "You're not going to ask for your money back, are you?"

"No," Claire said. "I just heard there might be some ghosts here. That's all."

"We have had a bit of a ghost problem," Irwin admitted. "At first we thought it was good for business. People wanted to see the ghosts. But then when they saw one, they ran out of the theater and asked for their money back."

Kaz raised an eyebrow at Finn.

Finn shrugged. "Sometimes Dave and Conrad and I liked to put on a little show for the solids."

"We couldn't afford to give all those people their money back, so when a boy came in and claimed he could get rid of the ghosts, we hired him," Irwin said. "He was here yesterday and the day before. He came in with a big fan and blew the ghosts out. Then he told us to leave all the doors and windows open. He said if there were any more ghosts hiding in here, the wind would blow them out."

So that's what happened to Dave, Kaz thought. The boy probably blew him out of the theater the day before yesterday. Just like he blew Conrad and Jessie away today.

"Who is this boy?" Claire asked, one hand on her hip.

Irwin scratched his chin. "I'm not sure I remember his name. He wasn't much older than you, though. Wait, he had a card." Irwin felt in his pocket and pulled out a business card. He handed it to Claire. The card said *Gabriel Goodman, Ghost Sweeper*.

ANOTHER GHOST CATCHER

Kaz, Finn, and Little John hovered safely inside Claire's water bottle while Claire stood on the sidewalk outside the movie theater and stared at the card in her hand.

"There's an address on this card," Claire told her ghost friends. "I don't have to be home until dinnertime. We've got time to visit Gabriel Goodman before we go back to the library."

"Great! Let's go," Finn said.

"Wait," Kaz said as Claire started walking.

She stopped. "What?" she asked.

"Well," Kaz said. "If this boy can see ghosts when they're not glowing, then won't he be able to see *us*? What if he somehow forces us out of this bottle and blows us into the Outside, too?"

Little John let out a big breath of air. "Do you have to worry about every little thing, Kaz?"

"Of course he does," Finn said. "He's Kaz."

Claire set her bag on a bench, then sat down beside it. "No, Kaz is right to worry," she said, holding her water bottle on her lap. "We know this boy blew Jessie and Conrad out of the theater. He probably blew Dave out of the theater, too. We need to make sure you guys stay safe."

"We're safe. We're inside your water bottle," Finn said.

"It doesn't hurt to take extra precautions," Claire said. She unzipped her bag, picked up the bottle with the ghosts, and put it inside the bag.

"Hey!" Little John cried as Claire started to zip her bag closed over them.

Finn swam to the top of the bottle. "Don't put us in here!" he shouted. "We won't be able to see anything!"

"That means Gabriel won't be able to see you, either," Claire said. "I think that's best. At least until we know a little more about him." She zipped her bag the rest of the way closed and everything went dark around Kaz, Finn, and Little John.

Finn sighed. "Maybe she's right," he said. "Better safe than sorry. No one knows that better than me."

The ghosts could tell by the way the bottle jiggled back and forth that Claire was walking now. Kaz wondered how far away Gabriel's house was.

"This reminds me of when we traveled inside that box with the doll that didn't shrink," Little John said. He rubbed his hands together to make them glow, which provided a little light inside Claire's bag.

"Huh? What are you talking about?"

Finn asked. He rubbed his hands together, too.

Kaz and Little John told Finn about the doll they'd found in the secret room at the library. They thought it belonged to Little John's friend Kiley. They wanted to take it to her, but they couldn't make the doll shrink. That was when they learned that ghostly objects that used to be solid don't shrink.

By the time Kaz and Little John finished the story, it sounded as though

they had arrived at Gabriel's house. They could hear Claire talking to someone.

"I'm looking for Gabriel Goodman," she said. Her voice sounded muffled, but Kaz could still make it out.

"That's me," a boy replied. "I see you have my card. Do you have a ghost you need me to take care of?"

"No, I—" Claire broke off. "This is kind of hard to explain. Can I come in?"

"Okay," Gabriel said. The ghosts heard a door open, then shut.

"Let's go out there," Little John whispered. He started to pass through the water bottle into Claire's bag, but Kaz and Finn each grabbed one of his arms and pulled him back.

"Not yet," Kaz whispered back.

"Not until we know it's safe," Finn added.

"I'm like you," Claire said to Gabriel. "I can see ghosts when they're not glowing and I can hear ghosts when they're not wailing."

"What's glowing? What's wailing?" Gabriel asked.

"You don't know what glowing and wailing mean?" Claire asked. "Haven't you ever *talked* to any of the ghosts you've seen?"

"No. Why would I do that?" Gabriel said.

"Because that's how you get to know people," Claire said. "You talk to them. You tell them about yourself and they tell you about themselves. That's how you become friends."

"Why would I want to be friends with a ghost?" Gabriel asked.

Claire sighed. "Why *wouldn't* you

want to be friends with a ghost?" she asked. Then she told Gabriel about Kaz and his family, and how she and Kaz had formed a detective agency to find Kaz's missing family and to solve ghostly mysteries.

"So, when you solve these cases and you find new ghosts, you *don't* blow them outside like I do?" Gabriel asked.

"No," Claire said. "I bring them home with me. Or I take them someplace where they'll be happy."

"How do you do that?" Gabriel asked. "You can't take them outside. The wind blows them away."

Claire paused for a second. Then she said, "I'll show you. *If* you promise to be nice. You can't blow the ghosts outside or attack them in any way."

"You mean you've got some ghosts

with you right now?" Gabriel said.

"I do," Claire said. She started to unzip her bag and light poured in around Kaz, Finn, and Little John.

The ghosts blinked, squinted, and covered their eyes.

"Oh, wow." Gabriel breathed as Claire slowly lifted her water bottle from her bag. He was a teenager like Finn. He wore dark gray pants and a gray hoodie. His hair was long and uncombed.

"The medium-size ghost is my friend Kaz," Claire said. "The older one is his big brother, Finn, and the younger one is their little brother, Little John. Guys, this is Gabriel."

"Hello," Little John said. Finn raised a hand in greeting. None of them moved from the bottle.

"How'd they get so small? They're

76

like miniature ghosts," Gabriel said,
peering in at them.

"You don't know much about ghosts,
do you?" Claire asked. "They can shrink
and expand and pass through walls.
And most people can't see them when
they do that, which helps when you're
a detective. My friend Kaz can even
transform stuff. That means he can turn
a solid object into a ghostly object."

"For real?" Gabriel looked at Kaz.
"Show me."

"Go ahead, Kaz," Claire said, motioning for him to come out of the bottle.

Kaz wasn't sure he should, but Claire seemed to think it was okay.

"We're with you, Kaz," Finn said as the three ghosts passed through the bottle and expa-a-a-anded BIGGER than their normal sizes.

Gabriel leapt backward.

Kaz looked around for something to transform. There was a fan on the floor. It looked about the same size as the handheld vacuum Claire used as her "ghostcatcher." Was that what Gabriel used to blow Jessie, Conrad, and Dave into the Outside? If so, that would be a good thing to transform.

Kaz swam over, put his thumbs and second fingers on the fan, and *POOF!* The fan turned ghostly.

"Wow!" Gabriel said, his eyes open wide. "C-can you put it back?"

"He can," Finn said, swimming in front of Kaz. "But he's not going to. Not until you tell us what happened to Jessie, Conrad, and Dave. Did you blow them out of the movie theater?" Finn expanded even larger. He was twice Gabriel's size now.

"Who are all those people he's talking about?" Gabriel asked Claire.

"The ghosts at the movie theater," Claire replied. "Did you blow them outside?"

Gabriel swallowed hard. "I-I blew *some* ghosts out of the movie theater," he admitted. "Yesterday and the day before. But it was a job. I'm sorry. I didn't know they were your friends. I didn't know you could be friends with ghosts. Please, don't hurt me." He covered his head with his arms.

Finn snorted. "We're not going to hurt you," he said.

"But we want you to help us find our ghost friends," Kaz said. "Will you do that?"

"Yes." Gabriel nodded. "Yes, I'll help. But I don't know what happened to them. I blew them through that big window at the front of the theater and then the wind took them."

"We'll find them," Claire said confidently. "I know we will."

80

CHAPTER 7
EVERYONE MAKES MISTAKES

'm home!" Claire called as she and Gabriel thundered up the stairs. "And I brought a friend. His name is Gabriel."

Friend *might be stretching it a little,* Kaz thought as he and his brothers passed through Claire's water bottle.

Claire's mom poked her head out from the kitchen. "Oh, hello," she said. "Dinner will be ready in about half an hour. Will you stay for dinner, Gabriel?"

"Sure," Gabriel said with a shrug.

Claire's mom smiled and returned to the kitchen. Then Kaz's parents and dog wafted *out* of the kitchen.

"You must've put up a lot of those flyers," Kaz's mom said. "You've been gone all afternoon."

"More ghosts?" Gabriel said, staring at Kaz's parents.

"Woof! Woof!" Cosmo barked. He sniffed Gabriel's ear. Gabriel tried to brush him away, but his hand passed through the ghost dog.

"How many ghosts do you know, anyway?" Gabriel asked Claire.

"Lots," she said. She unzipped her bag and pulled out her notebooks.

Little John pointed at the green one. "That notebook is full of ghosts she knows," he said.

Kaz's mom wafted closer. "Who is this

solid boy?" she asked, looking Gabriel over from head to toe. "What does he mean 'more ghosts'? Can he see us, too?"

"Yes," Kaz said.

"His name is Gabriel," Little John said. "The guy at the movie theater hired him to get rid of the ghosts."

"Oh, no," Mom said. She put her hand to her mouth.

"Oh, yes," Finn said. "He blew Dave away from the theater two days ago and then yesterday he came back and blew Jessie and Conrad away."

Gabriel looked down at the floor and shifted from one foot to the other while Finn talked.

"So, now they're missing, too?" Mom said. "Why in the world did you bring this boy *here*?"

"Because he's sorry," Little John said.

Just then, Beckett's head rose through the floor. Gabriel jumped out of the way.

"I want to help find your friends," Gabriel said to all the ghosts.

"You should've thought of that before you blew them away," Mom said, shaking her finger at Gabriel. "Do you have any idea how much trouble you've caused? It's extremely dangerous for ghosts to be

in the Outside." She expanded larger and larger with every word she spoke. "It's like you being in a tornado! Have you ever been in a tornado? Have you ever lost loved ones?"

Solid people can't shrink, but somehow Gabriel looked smaller than he did before. His bottom lip quivered.

"Mom, chill," Finn said.

"Yeah, everyone makes mistakes," Kaz said.

Mom looked at Finn. Then at Beckett.

Embarrassed, Beckett quickly disappeared beneath the floor.

Mom looked a little embarrassed, too. "How are you going to find the ghosts that you blew away?" she asked Gabriel as she shrunk to her normal size. Her tone of voice was a little nicer, but not a lot.

"We're open to suggestions," Claire said. "From everyone. Even you, Beckett." She raised her voice so he could hear her through the floor.

Beckett's head popped back in. "Really?" he said. "You want my help, too?"

"The more people we have helping, the more likely we are to find the lost ghosts," Mom said to Beckett.

Beckett drifted up, up, up until his whole body was in Claire's living room. But he still kept some distance between himself and Kaz's mom.

"Okay, who's got an idea for how we can find Dave, Jessie, and Conrad?" Little John asked as Claire and Gabriel sat down on the couch.

No one seemed to have one.

"I could ask my parents if they have any ideas. They're private detectives," Claire told Gabriel.

"Do they know that you can see ghosts?" Gabriel asked.

"Yes," Claire said. "What about your parents? Do they know about you?"

"They know, but they don't understand," Gabriel said with a sad smile. "I'm not even sure they believe me when I say it."

Claire nodded knowingly. "My mom saw ghosts when she was a kid, but she doesn't see them anymore. And I didn't know she used to see them at first. I told her about the ghosts I saw and she said,

'There's no such thing as ghosts.' Even though she knew from her own childhood that that wasn't true. She stopped seeing them and she thought I'd stop seeing them, too, if I just ignored them. But then we talked about it more and now she understands."

"I don't think my parents ever saw ghosts when they were kids. They think this is a phase I'll grow out of," Gabriel said.

"How old are you?" Claire asked.

"Twelve," Gabriel said. "How old are you?"

"Ten," Claire replied. "I started seeing ghosts a year ago. When I was nine."

"Me too," Gabriel said. "I mean, I was nine when I first started seeing them, too. I ignored them at first, but they never went away. Not unless I made them go away."

The ghosts cringed when Gabriel said that.

Gabriel shifted on the couch. "People don't believe you can see ghosts if they've never seen one themselves," he said. "But if they have seen one, then they want your help getting rid of it. You can make a lot of money getting rid of ghosts!"

"Not everyone wants their ghosts to go away," Claire said. "And you don't have to blow them away. You can bring them here."

"Or if they're old, you can bring them to Valley View," Little John piped in. "There are lots of old ghosts there."

"A lot of the solid people who live there can see the ghosts. They play cards together," Kaz added.

"Huh," Gabriel said. "Where else do ghosts live? We know there are a bunch here at the library, and apparently at Valley View, too. There used to be three at the movie theater—"

"Four," Little John interrupted.

"Yeah, there's still one at the movie theater," Finn said to Gabriel. "His name's George. You missed him both times you were there."

Gabriel gave Finn a nervous half smile, then turned to Claire. "We should like, map out the town or something," he said. "Find out if there are parts of

town where there are more ghosts and parts where there aren't any. Maybe that would tell us where the wind blows the ghosts."

"That's a good idea," Claire said as she turned to a new page in her notebook.

"You'll need a bigger piece of paper than that," Gabriel said. "Maybe we should look for a map of the town. We can mark on it where we know there are ghosts. If we can find a map."

"We could download one from the Internet," Claire said.

"Or you could go downstairs and find one," Beckett said. "You are in a library, after all."

"You want us to write in a book?" Claire asked. "I don't think my grandma would like that very much."

Just then, Claire's cell phone rang. She

pulled it out of her pocket and checked the display. "Hmm. I don't know that number," she said with a frown. She put the phone to her ear and said, "Hello?"

The person on the other end talked so loud that everyone in the room could hear her. "Hello? Is this C & K Ghost Detectives? I just saw your sign on a lamppost at the end of my street. I'm calling because I think I've got your ghost in my house!"

CHAPTER 8

WHO'S IN CHARGE?

Your ghost, the woman said. Not *a* ghost.

"She found Dave!" Kaz said as soon as Claire hung up the phone. The other ghosts gathered around.

"We're about to find out," Claire said. But then she remembered something. "Oh no. Mom said dinner would be ready in half an hour. She might not let me go now. I should've asked before I told this lady we'd be right over."

"Your mom *has* to let you go," Kaz's mom said. "This could be our chance to find Dave. If you don't go now, he might leave. Or be blown away. Let me talk to your mother. Mom to Mom." She swam toward the kitchen.

Kaz and Claire exchanged a look.

"How can that ghost talk to your mom?" Gabriel asked Claire. "You said she saw ghosts when she was a kid, but she doesn't see them anymore."

"Duh! Our mom can glow!" Finn said.

"Oh. Right," Gabriel said. "Well, if she still says no, I could check it out for you. Let me borrow your water bottle and I'll bring the ghost back here."

"When you're the one who blew him outside in the first place?" Finn said. "I don't think so."

"I'm not sure a ghost would go

with you, son," Pops said.

"He might if a couple of you came with me," Gabriel said to Kaz and the other ghosts. "You could show him we're friends."

Were *they friends?* Kaz wondered. Could the ghosts trust that Gabriel wouldn't blow them into the Outside? Maybe. But still, he would rather travel with Claire than Gabriel. Just to be safe.

Claire's mom walked into the room. Kaz's mom drifted beside her, the glow fading from her body.

"Kaz's mom and I just had a little talk," Claire's mom said to Claire and Gabriel.

"Have you two talked to each other before?" Claire asked.

"Oh, yes. Many times," Claire's mom said. Kaz's mom nodded in agreement.

"When?" Kaz and Claire asked at the same time, each one looking at his or her own mother. Kaz's mom hadn't been at the library *that* long.

"When you're not around," Claire's mom said, ruffling her hair.

"What do you talk about?" Kaz asked.

His mom made a face that said she wasn't going to tell him what they talked about and that he should listen to Claire's mom right now.

"I know about that phone call you received a few minutes ago," Claire's mom said. "Kaz's mom thinks there's

a possibility her long-lost brother is at this woman's house right now."

"That's right," Claire said. "The lady's name is Mrs. Sweet. She doesn't live far from here." Claire held up a scrap of paper where she'd written down the address. "I know it's almost dinnertime. Can I go?"

"Yes," Claire's mom replied. "But Kaz's mom will go with you."

Claire tilted her head. "You say that like Kaz's mom is going to be *in charge* of me."

Both moms smiled. "That's because she is," Claire's mom said.

* * * * * * * * * * * * * *

Kaz, his mom, and Finn traveled to Mrs. Sweet's house inside Claire's water bottle. Gabriel went with them, too. Little John, Pops, and Beckett stayed at the library with Cosmo.

97

Mrs. Sweet's house was small and white with blue trim. There was no grass in the front yard. Just flowers, bushes, and trees.

Claire and Gabriel walked up to the front door and rang the bell. A woman around Claire and Kaz's moms' age came to the door. She wore a white shirt that was splattered with paint, and her jeans were rolled up to her knees.

"You must be C & K Detectives," the woman said as she opened the door. "Which one of you is the C and which one is the K?"

"I'm Claire, so I'm the C," Claire said as she stepped inside. She glanced uneasily at Kaz inside her water bottle.

"I guess that makes me the K," Gabriel said with a nervous laugh. He did not offer his name and Mrs. Sweet didn't ask.

"Come on in," Mrs. Sweet led Claire and Gabriel into the living room. Large sheets of plastic covered the furniture and the floor. Mrs. Sweet had obviously been painting the wall behind the couch.

"I like that color," Claire said, gazing at the dark green wall.

Mrs. Sweet smiled. "Thank you. I saw your ghost when I was putting the first coat of paint on this wall."

Kaz, Finn, and Mom passed through Claire's water bottle. Right in front of Mrs. Sweet. She clearly didn't see *them*. She went on with her story. "I dipped my brush in the paint and all of a sudden this ghost appeared in midair. Right in front of my face!"

"Was it glowing?" Gabriel asked.

"Glowing?" Mrs. Sweet looked confused.

"Don't!" Kaz raised a warning finger to Finn. They were here to find Dave, not to scare Mrs. Sweet.

Finn put his hand to his chest and lifted his eyebrow as though to say, *Who me?*

"It's what ghosts do when they want people like us to see them," Claire said.

"Now that you mention it, he did have kind of a bluish glow to him," Mrs. Sweet

said. "He was not a happy ghost, let me tell you!"

"That's . . . because . . . you . . . jammed . . . a . . . paintbrush . . . through . . . my . . . stomach!" a ghostly voice wailed from the other room.

Everyone turned.

"Dave? Is that you?" Mom called. She swam toward the voice.

"Sorry, Mom," Finn said. "But that's not Dave's voice."

No, it's not, Kaz thought. He knew exactly whose voice it was.

CHAPTER 9

WAIT A MINUTE...

onrad!" Finn exclaimed as the solid people walked and the ghost people swam into the next room.

Conrad hovered above the dining room table. "Dude! What are you guys doing here?" he asked.

"We came to rescue you," Kaz said.

"Then why do you look so surprised to see me?" Conrad asked.

"We thought we were rescuing Dave," Mom said, trying not to sound disappointed.

"You both heard someone say 'that's because you jammed a paintbrush through my stomach,' didn't you?" Mrs. Sweet said to Claire and Gabriel. Conrad had wailed those words, so Mrs. Sweet heard them. But she hadn't heard anything the ghosts said after that. And she couldn't see any of them, either.

"ACK!" Conrad shrieked when he noticed Gabriel. He shot up to a corner of the ceiling.

"Do you see the ghost?" Mrs. Sweet asked Claire and Gabriel. She still thought there was only one ghost in her house.

"Yeah. He's up there." Gabriel pointed at Conrad.

Conrad stayed where he was, but expaaaanded his arm and finger toward Gabriel. "That's the guy who attacked me and Jessie!" he told the other ghosts.

"He came with this big fan and blew Jessie and me out the front window of the movie theater. He probably blew Dave out, too. If you're here to rescue me, why did you bring him with you?"

Mrs. Sweet squinted up at the corner of the ceiling. "How come you two can see him and I can't?"

"Because he's not glowing," Gabriel said. "We can see ghosts when they're not glowing. Most people can't."

Mrs. Sweet looked like she wasn't sure whether or not to believe that.

Gabriel turned to Claire. "How are we going to get him down from there?"

"Why don't you back up a little and let me handle it." Claire gave Gabriel a gentle push. "He's kind of scared of you."

Mrs. Sweet chuckled. "The ghost is scared of us?"

"Not all of us. Just him," Claire said, tipping her head toward Gabriel. "Because he and the ghost got off on the wrong foot at the movie theater."

"A guy at the theater hired me to come in and get rid of the ghosts," Gabriel tried to explain. "It was a job."

Claire turned to Conrad. "Gabriel wants you to know that he's sorry for the way he did that job," she said. "He won't ever blow any ghosts outside again. He wanted to help us find you. He wants to find Jessie and Dave, too, and take you all someplace safe."

"I don't know," Conrad said, keeping a wary eye on Gabriel.

Mrs. Sweet shook her head in confusion. "What's happening here?"

Claire raised her water bottle to Conrad.

"I'll take you wherever you want to go," she promised. "Back to the movie theater, if you want. George is still there. We can pick him up and I can take you all to the library, if you want. You'll be safe there. Then we can try and find Jessie and Dave."

"You can trust Claire," Kaz said to Conrad. "You may not trust Gabriel, but you can trust Claire." To prove it, he shrank down . . . down . . . down . . . and swam into Claire's water bottle.

"Yeah. Come on, Conrad," Finn said as he and Mom shrank down . . . down . . . down . . . and followed Kaz. "Unless you'd rather stay here by yourself?"

"No. We need to find Jessie and Dave," Conrad said. "I don't know what happened to Dave, but I *do* know what happened to Jessie. Will she really help us?" He gestured toward Claire.

"Yes," Kaz and Finn said at the same time.

Conrad shrank down . . . down . . . down . . . and joined the other ghosts inside the water bottle.

"Okay," Claire said to Mrs. Sweet. "I've got your ghost in here." She patted her water bottle.

"She does," Gabriel said. "I can see it."

Mrs. Sweet scratched her ear. "Well, thank you," she said. "I think."

* * * * * * * * * * * * * * * * * *

"What happened to Jessie?" Kaz asked Conrad. The four ghosts hovered inside Claire's water bottle while Claire and Gabriel walked away from Mrs. Sweet's house.

"I saw her blow into a car that was

parked in front of the movie theater," Conrad said. He drifted to the edge of the bottle and peered up at Claire. "Please! You have to take us to the movie theater."

Claire held her water bottle so she could see and talk to the ghosts better. "Okay," she said. "But you guys blew away yesterday. That car probably isn't parked there anymore."

"It might be," Conrad said.

"It's worth a try, isn't it?" Mom asked.

"Sure," Claire said. She put the strap over her shoulder and let the water bottle dangle at her side. Right between her and Gabriel.

"Um, excuse me?" Conrad called to Claire. "Would you mind moving us to your *other* shoulder?"

"What do you think I'm going to

do?" Gabriel yelled at the ghosts. "Open her water bottle and dump you out?"

A solid lady who was pushing a stroller across the street shot Gabriel a strange look.

"You never know," Conrad said.

Claire moved her water bottle to her other shoulder. And a few minutes later, they were downtown.

"I don't see any ghosts inside any of the cars parked out front," Claire said as they approached the movie theater. "Is the car you saw Jessie blow into still here, Conrad?"

Conrad peered around one of the stars on Claire's water bottle. "I don't see it," he said, disappointed.

Claire and Gabriel stopped walking.

"What should we do now?" Claire asked, leaning against the mailbox in front of the theater. "Should we go inside and get George?"

"I think we should wait here for that car to come back," Conrad said. He shook his head sadly. "I don't know why Jessie let go of my hand. We were holding hands when Gabriel turned on the fan. And we were still holding hands when we passed through that mailbox. But then she let go, and she floated into a car that was parked right over there." He pointed to where a black pickup truck was parked now. "I tried to swim to the car, too, but I floated up and over all these buildings, and into that lady's house where you found me."

"Wait a minute," Kaz said, staring at the mailbox. "Did you say you passed through the mailbox?"

"Yes. Why?" Conrad asked.

"I wonder if Dave passed through it, too?" Kaz said. He glanced at the large window behind the mailbox. "In fact, if Gabriel turned on the fan right there . . ." He pointed. "Then it's possible he blew Dave into the mailbox rather than into the Outside!"

"That is about where I was standing when I turned the fan on," Gabriel said. "Both days."

Kaz hovered at the edge of the bottle and craned his neck so he could see Claire. "Hey, Claire!" he called. "Would you hold your water bottle up against the mailbox? I want to see if Dave's in there."

CHAPTER 10

FOUND!

No, Kaz!" his mom said. "It's too dangerous. What if you miss the bottle when you come back? You could blow away!"

"I'm not going to pass my whole self through," Kaz said. "Just my head. So I can see if Dave's in there. Hold my legs, please."

Claire held her bottle tight against the mailbox. Kaz started to pass his head through, but Mom pulled him back. "*I'll*

114

see if Dave is in there," she said. "You boys hold *my* legs."

"It can't be that dangerous if Kaz is willing to do it," Finn muttered as Mom swam headfirst through Claire's water bottle and into the mailbox. Kaz and Finn each held one of her legs. They had to hold on tight because all of a sudden she started kicking and flailing around.

"Mom? Are you okay?" Kaz asked. He wished he could see into the mailbox, too.

"You have to shrink more!" Mom said. Her voice sounded hollow and far away. "Smaller! As small as I am."

Who was Mom talking to? Was Kaz right? Was Dave in there? Or Jessie?

The three ghost boys *sloooowly* pulled Mom back into Claire's water bottle. And Mom pulled another ghost in with her.

115

"Dave!" Finn and Conrad cried when he finally popped through the edge of the bottle. Everyone had to shrink a little smaller to make room for Dave.

Mom stared at Dave. "A-are you . . . ?" Mom asked. She couldn't even finish the sentence.

Dave rubbed his eyes and stared at Mom. "Are *you* . . . ?" He couldn't finish his sentence, either.

"Dave?" Finn said, squeezing in between his mom and his friend. "This is my mom, Elise, and my brother Kaz."

"Elise?" Dave said. He couldn't seem to take his eyes off her. "You're all grown up!"

"So are you!" Mom said.

Finn's friend Dave *was* their Uncle Dave! They were the same person.

Amazing, Kaz thought as he watched

his mom and Uncle Dave hug each other.

Finally, Mom pulled away. "You're bald!" She laughed.

"Not completely," Dave said. He felt the short curls above his ear and at the nape of his neck. "Hey, where's my cap?" He looked all around.

"Where did you even get that cap, anyway?" Conrad asked. "It was ugly!"

"It was not," Dave protested. "It was a Minnesota Twins cap. A Minnesota Twins cap is *never* ugly. I found it years ago. In the lost and found in there." He pointed at the movie theater. "It used to be solid, but I transformed it."

"You can transform stuff?" Kaz cried out.

"Yes," Dave said, looking at Kaz for the first time.

"So can I!" Kaz said. "I'm the only

one in the whole family who can!"

"Yeah, but you still can't glow," Finn muttered.

Dave puffed up his chest. "You must get your transformation skill from me," he said proudly.

Kaz's mom touched Dave's bald head. He swatted her hand away. "I sure wish I knew what happened to my cap," he said. "It fell off when I was inside that mailbox. When I tried to put it back on, it kept falling over my eyes. So I just held it in my hand. I must've dropped it when you took my hands, Elise."

"Did you shrink when you were in the mailbox?" Kaz asked. He'd never seen Uncle Dave full-size, so he didn't know how big he was.

"A little," Dave replied.

"That's probably why your cap kept falling over your eyes. It didn't fit after you shrank," Kaz explained. "You can't shrink or expand something that's been transformed. You know that, right?"

"Uh . . . ," Uncle Dave said. "I'm not sure I did know that. I don't think I've ever tried to shrink or expand something I transformed before." He gazed sadly at the mailbox. "How will I ever get my cap back? If I can't shrink it, I can't bring it inside this bottle."

Conrad snorted. "Just leave it, dude."

"Claire can come back with a big box sometime," Little John suggested.

"One that's big enough to hold your cap."

"Who's Claire?" Dave asked.

The other ghosts pointed at Claire outside the bottle. She waved at Dave. Gabriel stood silently beside her.

Dave gasped. He pointed at Gabriel. "Th-that's the guy who blew me out of the movie theater!" he told the other ghosts.

"We know," Conrad and Finn said together.

"We've got a lot to talk about," Mom said, patting her brother on the arm.

"A lot." Kaz nodded in agreement. Where would they even begin?

* * * * * * * * * * * * * * * *

"I don't want to go to the library with you guys," Conrad said as Claire and Gabriel moved away from the mailbox.

"I'd rather stay here in case Jessie comes back. Would you please take me inside the movie theater?"

"Sure," Claire said, checking the time on her phone. "Do you want me to take you all the way in or can I just put my bottle up against the window so you can pass through?"

"The window will be fine," Conrad said.

"George will be happy to see you," Finn said. "He was really scared when we were here before."

"Last we saw, he was in the men's room," Kaz said.

"Maybe you shouldn't let the solid people see or hear you for a while," Mom told Conrad. "You don't want them to call someone else to come and blow you away."

"I'll lay low," Conrad said. "Thanks for the ride home!" He passed through Claire's water bottle and waved good-bye.

Then Claire and Gabriel took the other ghosts back to the library. Pops, Little John, Cosmo, and Beckett were waiting for them in the entryway.

"Well?" Pops said as soon as Claire shut the door. The ghosts passed through Claire's water bottle.

"Look! There's a new ghost with them!" Little John exclaimed.

"Woof! Woof!" Cosmo barked. He sniffed Uncle Dave all over.

"I'd like you all to meet my brother, Dave," Mom said cheerfully.

"Pleasure," Pops said, shaking Dave's hand.

"Hooray! We have a new uncle!" Little

John said, throwing his arms around Dave's middle.

Beckett hung back.

Dave squinted at him. "Beckett? Is that you, old buddy? You got old!"

"You too," Beckett said. "D-do you still think of me as your friend?"

"Of course," Dave said. He wafted over and squeezed Beckett's shoulders. "What happened all those years ago was an accident. I don't hold any grudges."

"Thanks, old buddy," Beckett said as he hugged Dave in return.

If Uncle Dave didn't hold any grudges, maybe Mom, Grandmom, and Grandpop could forgive Beckett, too. Maybe they could all be friends.

"We'll have to take you to see Mom and Dad," Mom said to Uncle Dave. She meant Grandmom and Grandpop.

"Tomorrow," said Claire as she led Gabriel toward the stairs. "It's past dinnertime and Gabriel and I are starving!"

"Hmph," Beckett said. "Solids. Always wanting to eat something."

"Wait, solid girl!" Dave called after her.

Claire turned. "Do *not* call me solid girl," she warned.

"Call her Claire," Kaz said.

"Okay." Dave cleared his throat. "*Claire*, if we're going out again tomorrow, would you kindly take me back to that mailbox inside a larger box so I may retrieve my cap?"

"Yes," Claire said. "As long as you call me Claire and not solid girl."

"Maybe we can also find out whether Jessie came back to the movie theater," Little John said.

"And *then* maybe you can all come back to my house and Kaz can make my fan solid again," Gabriel said. "You said you could do that, right?"

The ghosts looked at one another.

Finn winked at Kaz, then turned to Gabriel. "Actually, I'm the one who told

you that," he said. "But I think I was mistaken. I don't think Kaz knows how to make your fan solid again. He has lots of trouble with his ghost skills."

"*Lots* of trouble," Little John added.

"Your fan may have to stay ghostly forever," Kaz said with a shrug. "Sorry."

DON'T MISS THE OTHER BOOKS IN THE HAUNTED LIBRARY SERIES!

THE GHOST IN THE ATTIC

THE GHOST BACKSTAGE

THE FIVE O'CLOCK GHOST

THE SECRET ROOM

THE GHOST AT THE FIRE STATION

THE GHOST IN THE TREE HOUSE

THE HIDE-AND-SEEK GHOST